PATRICIA POLACCO
The Trees of the Dancing Goats

Aladdin Paperbacks

New York London Toronto Sydney Singapore

ALSO BY PATRICIA POLACCO

Babushka's Doll

The Keeping Quilt

My Rotten Redheaded Older Brother

Some Birthday!

In loving memory of my hero . . . my mother, Mary Gaw Barber,
August 8, 1913–May 13, 1996

First Aladdin Paperbacks edition October 2000

Copyright © 1996 by Patricia Polacco

Aladdin Paperbacks

An imprint of Simon & Schuster Children's Publishing Division

1230 Avenue of the Americas

New York, NY 10020

Also available in a Simon & Schuster Books for Young Readers hardcover edition

Designed by Anahid Hamparian

The text for this book was set in 14-point Life.

The illustrations were rendered in marking pens and pencil.

Printed and bound in China

10 9

The Library of Congress has cataloged the hardcover edition as follows:

Polacco, Patricia. The trees of the dancing goats / Patricia Polacco.   p.   cm.

Summary: During a scarlet-fever epidemic one winter in Michigan, a Jewish family helps make Christmas special

for their sick neighbors by making their own Hanukkah miracle.

ISBN 0-698-80862-3 (hc.)

[1. Hanukkah—Fiction. 2. Christmas—Fiction. 3. Jews—Fiction. 4. Grandparents—Fiction. 5. Russian Americans—Fiction.] I. Title

PZ7.P75186Tr   1996

[E]--dc20   95-26670

ISBN 0-689-83857-3 (Aladdin pbk.)

1109 PXA

Aᴛ ᴏᴜʀ ғᴀʀᴍ just outside Union City, Michigan, we didn't celebrate the same holidays as most of our neighbors . . . but we shared their delight and anticipation of them just the same.

"Such cold the winter brings," my Babushka said, as she looked out our front window. "My bones it makes to ache." She slapped her chest. Then she caught my eye and winked.

She wasn't fooling me. I knew how much she loved the snow. It reminded her of her homeland in the Ukraine.

"Carl'e, again you complain, but still you watch the snow with such light in your eyes," Grampa said, and he threw her a kiss.

My grandfather was from Soviet Georgia, way to the south of Russia. He and Babushka spoke Russian and had wonderful accents. They kept their homelands in their hearts, even though they would never be permitted to return.

Just then, Momma rolled into the long driveway.

"Momma's home! Momma's home!" my brother, Richard, called as we watched her get out of the car.

Momma drove way over to Battle Creek every day to teach school. But now she would be off for two weeks because of the holiday season. I loved having her home for winter vacation. This year we would have a week together to prepare, and then eight days of Hanukkah festivities.

The next day, Momma took out our old, tarnished menorah and asked me to polish it. While I rubbed, I watched my grandmother make the candles that we would put in it. Babushka tied long strings to a metal rod and dipped them into a pot of melted beeswax that she kept on the stove. Then she hung the wax-covered strings on the wall to dry before dipping them again to add another layer of wax. She hummed as she dipped, never seeming to tire of the long process.

Grampa prepared for our festival of lights as well. He carved small toys out of wood. Richard and I weren't supposed to know that he was making them for us.

But he did every year, and that afternoon, when he went to town, we couldn't help sneaking into his workroom to take a peek.

"Look, a dancing goat!" my brother exclaimed as he held one up.

"I like this one," I said, cradling a little dog in my palm.

Grampa had painted the animals with colors from his homeland. We marveled at how magical they all were.

"Do you think he made enough for all eight days of Hanukkah?" Richard asked as he eyed the array of wooden figures.

"You know he has," I whispered. I took one lasting look, knowing that soon Grampa would wrap them up in colored paper.

My mother called for me, and I thought she had caught us spying. But she only wanted me to go over to the Kremmels for some cornmeal. The Kremmels, our nearest neighbors, lived half a mile down the road. They were farmers, like us, and at harvesttime Mr. Kremmel always helped Grampa. All the neighbors helped each other that way. "Friendship means something," Grampa always said. "Especially for those who till the soil."

I practically lived at the Kremmels' house because Cherry Kremmel was my very best friend. We especially loved the holiday season, when I'd watch her family decorate their Christmas tree, and she'd watch my family light our menorah. I knew as we were bustling in anticipation of the festival of lights at our house, the Kremmels would be preparing for the arrival of Christmas at theirs.

But when I got there, I found everybody quite sick. Even Cherry, who was usually "full of *spizerinkto*," as my Babushka would say, seemed quiet and weak.

She was crying. "I hope Santa will remember where we live," she wailed.

"Well, why wouldn't he?" I asked.

"'Cause we haven't put up a tree this year, or even decorated. Papa's too sick to get out of bed and go chop one down." Then she coughed an awful cough.

I ran home and burst into our house with the news about Cherry and her family.

Momma seemed very worried.

"Did you go inside their house, Trisha?" she asked me.

"Sure," I answered.

"Uh-oh," my brother said.

They all looked at each other.

"When your grandfather was in town today," Babushka said very slowly, "Doctor Leach told him that many families around here have come down with scarlet fever."

"The Kremmels must have it—and I sent you there!" my mother said as she rushed me to the bathroom, pulled off my clothes, and soundly scrubbed every inch of me.

"Am I gonna get it, Momma?" I asked.

"It's very contagious," she answered. "We'll know in a few days."

"Am I gonna die?" I asked, starting to cry.

"No, baby," Momma said softly as she held me close. "But if you have it, it will make you quite sick."

For the next few days my family watched me carefully.

Richard, of course, took pleasure in making me feel like I was quarantined. He held a cloth over his mouth and nose every time he came near me. Then he'd hack and gag, mimicking the dreadful cough of the fever.

As the days passed, it was evident that I was not going to get sick. But more and more reports came to us of neighbors falling ill—the Everests, the Govlocks, the Tundervalds, the Moleskys. It was an epidemic.

We were all worried about our friends, but Babushka was determined that our festival of lights would go on as planned. On the afternoon before Hanukkah, she bustled around her kitchen. "Such *latkes* I'll make this year," she exclaimed while digging for the choicest potatoes in the bin. She hummed happily as she placed the potatoes in front of me. I shredded them with great care. They had to be just right for my Babushka's latkes. Momma and Babushka dressed down two chickens for roasting and put them in the oven.

Just as the aroma of the wonderful feast met our nostrils, the sun set, and it was time to light the menorah. Grampa recited the blessings and lit the *shommas*, the candle used to light all the others. Babushka put the first candle in the menorah and lit it with the shommas. Then Momma told the story, as she did every year, of our people long ago.

"Tonight we are celebrating miracles," she started. "The miracle that a very small band of Jewish farmers turned soldiers could defeat a huge Syrian army."

"Were they really farmers before they were soldiers?" Richard asked.

"Simple farmers," Grampa answered. "Just like us."

"They were fighting so that they could worship in their own way," my mother added.

"Then there was the miracle of the light," my grandfather said with a twinkle in his eye. "One little tiny drop of oil burned in the temple for eight days."

"Such a miracle!" my Babushka exclaimed.

"Miracles can happen even today," Grampa said quietly.

After dinner, Grampa handed us the first of our beautifully wrapped presents. He looked troubled, though.

"You know," he began, "our neighbors are having such a hard time, and this should be a time of gladness for them. If only we could do something to make their holiday special . . ." his voice trailed off.

Babushka thought for a while. "They always bring a tree into their house—only in America does a tree grow right out of a living room floor!" She rocked with laughter.

"Carl'e! We should cut down trees and take them into their houses!" Grampa announced. Babushka smiled in agreement.

"I'll cut them tonight. You can help, Richard," Grampa said, already pulling on his winter coat.

"We can dress down more chickens and take them food!" Babushka said as she scurried into the kitchen.

"Momma and I can decorate the trees!" I shouted excitedly.

"But this is not our custom—we have nothing to decorate the trees with," my grandmother said.

"What about the carvings?" my mother said softly.

They both looked at me. "What do you think? They have no way of making their children happy this year."

At first I was a little disappointed, but then, as I thought about it, I knew it was the right thing to do. Our neighbors needed cheering, and we were just about the only ones who didn't have the fever.

Grampa and Richard brought the cut trees into our living room. They nailed boards onto the bottom of each one so they would stand up.

They were very small trees—Grampa had only taken the tops off our evergreens—but they were beautiful, and when they were all standing in the living room, it looked like a forest.

"Like the woods just outside of Kiev when I was a little girl," Babushka said breathlessly.

Grampa started hanging some of his wooden animals on the branches of a tree. "A dancing goat," my Babushka remarked as she looked closely at one of them. "We shall call these . . . the trees of the dancing goats." We made sure to hang a dancing goat on each and every tree.

As we decorated the trees, we sang and laughed. The single candle in the menorah flickered as we rushed past it to reach another carved animal or to paste together paper chains to hang on the trees.

We all worked into the night. While Grampa, Richard, and I finished the decorating, Babushka and Momma roasted more chickens and fried more potato latkes. They packed the food in baskets and in each one Babushka put one of her homemade Hanukkah candles. "So they will have the light of God in their hearts . . . and so that God will protect them and make them well again," she murmured.

We loaded Grampa's old Ford with the trees and the food baskets and sent Babushka and Grampa into the early light of dawn with their Christmas cheer.

"Just like Santa," my brother said.

"Mr. and *Mrs.* Santa," I added.

We waited eagerly for their return later that morning. We thrilled when Babushka and Grampa told of how they entered the home of each neighbor, set up a tree in the living room, put the basket of food on the table, and then put a candle in a holder for them to light later. Momma was a little worried that they had been exposed to the fever, but Babushka said, "In so much worse I've been, you shouldn't know from. God will protect, God will protect . . . this I know!"

A week later, the eight days of Hanukkah had come and gone, and we sat down to have our last feast.

There was a knock at the door.

"Now who could that be?" Babushka said as she scurried to the door with her usual warm smile.

It was the Kremmels. Cherry and her mom and dad. They looked pale but assured us that they were quite well now.

"We have something for you!" Cherry announced as she bolted through the door, holding a basket.

Her mother and father had tears in their eyes as they hugged my grandparents and my mother.

"Look what my dad made for you!" Cherry said. She pulled out a menorah that Mr. Kremmel had carved out of wood. On it he had mounted some of the animals that we had given to them.

"How beautiful," my Babushka said as she placed it on our table.

"Come sit," Grampa invited them. "You are so welcome. Thank you! Thank you!"

"Thank *you*, George," Mr. Kremmel said, looking into Grampa's eyes.

They sat down and shared our feast. By this time our menorah had been lit for an hour or so, and when we lit the candles in the new menorah, we noticed something. Something wondrous.

"Look!" I called out. "Our old candles are exactly as tall as the new ones!"

"The old ones don't even look burned down," Momma said softly.

"Another miracle," Grampa said.

"A miracle, indeed," my Babushka said, giving me a big hug. Then we all got up and danced and laughed together in the flickering candlelight.

Our neighbors all recovered from that terrible fever. Few were left with any permanent damage. What they were left with was a long cherished memory of "that Christmas . . . when Santa really did come."

And my family, too, has never forgotten that incredible winter of the fever, the miracle of true friendship, and the trees of the dancing goats.